DEAR BAOBAB

WRITTEN BY CHERYL FOGGO

ILLUSTRATED BY QIN LENG

Second Story Press

On a wide street, in a city surrounded by low, rolling hills, a little spruce tree grew under the mailbox of a red brick house.

The boy who lived in the house liked to sit on the stone step beside the tree and listen to its voice. It sounded like someone singing his name.

"Ma–i–ko."

Maiko missed the giant baobab tree in his village in Africa, where he was born. He missed sitting in its shade eating cashews with the other children, who seemed not to notice that his ears stuck straight out from his head.

But Maiko didn't live among the baobabs anymore.

He lived in the red brick house now, with Uncle Peter and Auntie Ajia. Sometimes Uncle Peter and Maiko would walk to the forest of tall fir trees. Maiko would tip his head back and look up, so far up, and still he couldn't see the treetops.

"Uncle," he would ask, "How old are these trees?"

"Oh, about 400 years old," Uncle Peter would answer. Then, as though he knew what Maiko was thinking, he'd smile and say, "Not as old as your baobab."

Maiko's favorite baobab was more than 2,000 years old. "When this old baobab tree was a baby," his mother used to joke with him, "that tall mountain over there was just a pebble."

One morning, as Maiko sat in the fragrance of the little spruce, Uncle Peter joined him on the stone step.

"Uncle Peter," Maiko asked. "How old is this tree?"

"Oh, about seven years old," he replied, then paused. "What a strange place for a tree." He cupped Maiko's chin and went into the house.

After that, Maiko would say, "Hello tree, same age as me," on his way out and on his way in. Sometimes, he sat on the step and shared secrets that he told to no one else. He talked of his village and the baobabs, and how he missed his friends at the school where he had gone after his father and mother died. He told of how lonely he felt as the wind blew him across the wide ocean in an airplane, and how strange it was, at first, to sleep in the red brick house.

"But now," he said, "I fall asleep looking at the baobab that Aunt Ajia and I have painted on my bedroom wall."

Maiko told the tree about his new school, and about the boy, Leonard, who laughed at his ears.

As weeks passed in the city surrounded by low, rolling hills, Maiko learned many things from the spruce's song. He learned what it was like for a tree to have roots that sipped water hidden far beneath the earth, and how it felt to drink the sun and listen to the melodies of chickadees that sheltered in its branches. He learned how a tiny seed from a cone could float away to plant itself in the earth beneath the mailbox. And he learned that his ears were good, for only Maiko could hear the little tree when it sang.

One day, Maiko heard Uncle Peter and Aunt Ajia talking in the garden.

"Something will have to be done."

"It could crack the foundation."

And then, "What a strange place for a tree."

The wind sighed, and Maiko felt sad for the little tree that had been planted in the wrong place.

"Aunt Ajia," he asked that night after storytime, "What is a foundation?"

"Bones. The foundation holds up our house, just like your bones hold you up."

She switched on his nightlight and slipped away, leaving Maiko staring at the outline of the baobab in the near-dark.

Each day when he came home from school, Maiko was relieved to see the little tree still in its place beneath the mailbox.

Then, night began to come earlier and leaves from other trees fell, resting in the branches of the spruce.

For his first Halloween, Auntie Ajia invited Li, a boy from Maiko's class. Li was a wizard. Maiko was a baobab, made from a box, twenty-seven pipe cleaners, and green construction paper. Li taught him to shout "Trick-or-treat!"

On the street, they saw Leonard and he laughed and pointed at Maiko's ears. Maiko said, "I wish Leonard wouldn't laugh at my ears." But then Maiko remembered that his ears were good, because he could hear the spruce's song.

One day, as the last of the brown, crunchy leaves swirled around his feet, Maiko came home from school and found an ax and a saw lying on the stone step. He hid them in a dark place behind the shed, then sat down beside the little tree. "I want you to grow so tall that you can see across the ocean to my baobab, and tell her hello from me."

The spruce quivered.

"Please, grow your roots away from the bones," Maiko said.

That night as they ate a dinner of ugali and stew, Aunt Ajia was cross with Uncle Peter for leaving the cutting tools outside "for the whole world to steal." Though Maiko excused himself and went to bed, he did not sleep. The next morning, his heart felt gray. He listened, but could not hear the singing of the spruce.

As the wind blew colder and the days passed, Uncle Peter and Aunt Ajia seemed to have forgotten about the ax and the saw.

At school, Mrs. Croft taught the class songs about things Maiko didn't know, like skates, and snow, and sleigh bells. Maiko made sure to sit near Li in the music room, far from Leonard.

One day in December, on his way back from school, a cold, white jewel landed on Maiko's eyelash. He blinked. Many soft jewels were falling. When Maiko tried to touch them, they disappeared. He ran toward the red brick house, but stopped when he saw Uncle Peter with Aunt Ajia on the stone step, holding a new ax.

They waved, smiling, and Aunt Ajia called, "The little spruce will be our Christmas tree!"

Maiko ran. He raced along the wide street, and down the hill. Past the forest and up the other side, Maiko flew. His ears were cold, but he didn't care. He hated his ears and he hated the snow and the walls in his room and the songs about sleigh bells.

His mouth puffed small clouds. Maiko wondered how long it would take to run to the ocean, and how long it would take to cross, to get back home to Africa, where no one laughed at his ears, where he knew his baobab stood, strong and wide and safe.

Although Maiko was young, in his heart he knew many things. He knew that the tree could not do what he had asked it to do. He knew it was wrong to hide the ax and the saw. He knew what it meant to be small and planted in the wrong place.

Soon, Uncle Peter found him. They walked together, their footsteps muffled by the snow. After a time, Uncle Peter asked, "Why didn't you tell me how you felt about the tree?"

Maiko could not answer.

As though he knew about the bubble of sad feelings Maiko held inside, Uncle Peter said, "It's a serious thing, to feel that you don't belong." He looked down into Maiko's eyes and said, "It will get better, Nephew." They walked on.

Uncle Peter stopped and cupped Maiko's chin. "We won't cut down the tree," he said.

"But what about the foundation?" Maiko asked.

"We will find the answer."

Maiko felt the sadness bubble burst. He told Uncle Peter about how his dreams were filled with baobab trees, and he told him about Leonard.

An ebony curtain was falling as they talked about Leonard, and things they could do. By the time they reached the wide street, stars were winking above. Maiko's ears opened. He could hear the tree singing his name.

Just before Christmas, Maiko helped Aunt Ajia bake cookies shaped like baobab and spruce trees, and on Christmas morning, Li, in his new skates, pulled Maiko, on his new sled, along the frozen lagoon near the forest. They saw Leonard. He did not laugh at Maiko's ears.

The warm spring day of Maiko's eighth birthday, he sat on the stone step, waiting for Li and his father to come with their truck. Maiko told the tree its favorite story – about the day he and Uncle Peter found the Birthplace Forest. "People plant trees on their birthdays. You will be my tree," Maiko said. "You'll like it. Oh, you will grow so tall there – taller than the tallest tree in the forest where you were born."

Maiko heard the truck. "Uncle Peter," he shouted, "they are here to help us move my tree!"

Maiko looked at the little spruce. "I will come see you often, and when I do, I'll say, 'Hello, tree, same age as me.'" And then he whispered, "You see, we can't always grow where we are planted. But we still can grow somewhere else."

Library and Archives Canada Cataloguing in Publication

Foggo, Cheryl
Dear baobab / by Cheryl Foggo ; illustrated by Qin Leng.

ISBN 978-1-897187-91-3

I. Leng, Qin II. Title.

PS8561.O38D43 2011   jC813'.54   C2011-902610-4

Second Story Press gratefully acknowledges the support of the Ontario Arts Council and the Canada Council for the Arts for our publishing program. We acknowledge the financial support of the Government of Canada through the Book Publishing Industry Development Program.

Printed and bound in China

Published by
SECOND STORY PRESS
20 Maud Street, Suite 401
Toronto, Ontario, Canada
M5V 2M5
www.secondstorypress.ca

This book is dedicated to my buddies in life and literature — Miranda, Chandra and Clem.
—C.F.

For Lian, mom, and dad.
—Q.L.

A portion of the author's proceeds from the sale of this book will be donated to the Mary A. Tidlund Charitable Foundation. The Tidlund Foundation supports children like Maiko through projects that promote health, education and the alleviation of poverty in communities around the world.
www.tidlundfoundation.com